MY TEARS ARE IN HIS HANDS

UNVEILING THE WHOLENESS GOD HAS FOR YOU

TAMIKA D. ROBERSON

authorHOUSE

AuthorHouse™
1663 Liberty Drive
Bloomington, IN 47403
www.authorhouse.com
Phone: 833-262-8899

© 2021 Tamika D. Roberson. All rights reserved.

No part of this book may be reproduced, stored in a retrieval system, or transmitted by any means without the written permission of the author.

This is a work of fiction. All of the characters, names, incidents, organizations, and dialogue in this novel are either the products of the author's imagination or are used fictitiously.

Published by AuthorHouse 02/17/2021

ISBN: 978-1-6655-1742-3 (sc)
ISBN: 978-1-6655-1752-2 (e)

Print information available on the last page.

Any people depicted in stock imagery provided by Getty Images are models, and such images are being used for illustrative purposes only.
Certain stock imagery © Getty Images.

This book is printed on acid-free paper.

Because of the dynamic nature of the Internet, any web addresses or links contained in this book may have changed since publication and may no longer be valid. The views expressed in this work are solely those of the author and do not necessarily reflect the views of the publisher, and the publisher hereby disclaims any responsibility for them.

Scripture quotations marked AMP are from The Amplified Bible, Old Testament copyright © 1965, 1987 by the Zondervan Corporation. The Amplified Bible, New Testament copyright © 1954, 1958, 1987 by The Lockman Foundation. Used by permission. All rights reserved.

CONTENTS

Dedication vii
Preface ix

Chapter 1 The Love I Never Had............................... 1
Chapter 2 The Look In The Mirror 10
Chapter 3 The Secrets Kept...................................... 18
Chapter 4 The Battles Of Life.................................. 27
Chapter 5 The Breaking Point................................. 35
Chapter 6 The Workmanship Of God 40
Chapter 7 The Wait Will Be Great 46
Chapter 8 The Act Of Forgiveness 53

Appendix A.. 59
About the Author.. 65

DEDICATION

To all the extraordinary beautiful women. Yes, you, the one that is reading this book right now. I dedicate this book to everyone that selects this book in search of finding self-love and the immense power God has placed within you. I pray this book encourages you to; stand firm, confront your past, and conquer your pain. I want you to know that you are not alone. Life gets tough and sometimes knock us down faster than we can get up. But we will get through it together my dear. So here's to a new beginning, a new you and a new life. I need you to firmly declare "I am God's Masterpiece".

This book is also dedicated to my phenomenal mother, Beverly Bridges. You are definitely one of a kind. Thank you for your love, support and morals you instilled in me. Thank you for teaching me responsibility early in life. Thank you for being a shoulder to cry on. Thank you for being their every step of the way and never missing a beat. There are not enough words to describe just how important you are to me and what a powerful influence you continue to be. Because, of you, I shine!

Thank you for selecting this book and I pray this book encourages you to unveil the wholeness God has for you!

PREFACE

You see, something that is now broken was once whole. That's you. You are God's original design, but now, because of life's experiences, you find yourself broken. This is not God's perfect will for your life. He desires that you be made whole. You must rely on God alone for the healing and fulfillment you are seeking.

This story reflects the life of a young woman beginning with her childhood. As she began to experience the obstacles of life she is challenged with abandonment, low self-esteem, abuse, failures and sickness. She battles through life adversities and struggles to find her inner strength, just like many of us. Although this book takes us through painful experiences of life, you will also discover hope and encouragement and all the reasons of why you never give up. You must stop wasting time and energy looking for wholeness in the wrong places like romance, addictions, or even careers. You must realize that nothing and no one except God has the power to complete you as a person.

Don't live your life for other people. Instead, seek to please God by discovering and fulfilling his purposes for your life, no matter what other people think. Understand this: Thoughts that lead to brokenness are the devil's way of blocking what God wants you to know about who you are in Christ. Immediately destroy those negative thoughts about yourself. Allow your mind to listen to what God has to say about you. If you do, you will find wholeness. Are you ready to start believing and declaring what God says about you?

CHAPTER 1

THE LOVE I NEVER HAD

"A little girl needs her daddy to love her with gentlemanly charm, to hold her tightly when she is afraid and keep her safe from harm."

~ by Kacee Harrington

"**K**ayla, Kayla are you listening?" Mrs. Martin said with distress. Kayla looked up at Mrs. Martin worriedly. She was standing in line at the school on their way to the stage. It was History Day, and every child has a part to play in the various historical events. Kayla had a role as well, but she wasn't nervous about that. She remembered her lines. She knew what she had to say when she got onto the stage.

"Is everything alright, dear?" Mrs. Martin looked down at her kindly. She knelt down so she could look into Kayla's eyes. Kayla looked worried for some reason. Mrs. Martin was quite astounded at seeing a frown on the face of a four-year-old child.

This was Kayla's last day in Pre-K, and today was the first event she had participated in. Kayla was one of the shy kids in the group. She had never taken the initiative to participate in any events previously held. She didn't have a habit of chatting away like some of the other girls her age. That was the reason Mrs. Martin had insisted she step up today. Kayla had worked very hard to learn everything for the event. But she seemed troubled at the moment.

"What's going on, Kayla?" She asked her. "Why are you worried?" Kayla looked at her silently but didn't answer. She just looked down. "Don't worry, dear. I am sure you will do great!" Mrs. Martin smiled cheerfully, pecked her on the cheek, and stood up to usher all children up the stairs and onto the stage.

Precious little, four-year-old girls climbed up onto the stage led by Mrs. Martin accompanied by amid thunderous applause from the audience. The girls bowed to the audience as they had practiced. One by one, each of the girls came forward and began presenting the lines they had prepared. Kayla stood in the middle of the line, not really paying attention to what was being said. Her eyes were surveying the audience looking for someone special. As she looked, a beautiful woman with dark brown hair waved at her from the crowd. It was her mother, Joyce. Kayla smiled at her widely and waved back. Then her eyes turned to the seat next to her, and her smile faltered. It was empty.

Chris Anderson, Kayla's father, had not come to attend this event and Kayla couldn't have been more disappointed. She had dreaded that since the start of the day. Reminiscing in a gaze, she was getting ready and preparing to leave for school, she had asked her father if he would be here to see her perform, and he had said, "Of course." She remembered it very clearly. Before she could control it, Kayla had tears in her eyes. Big thick tears were rolling down her face. She began crying very loudly as the girl next to her stepped forward and began saying the lines she had rehearsed. Mrs. Martin rushed to Kayla and tried to calm her down but she just couldn't. Kayla kept on crying until Mrs. Martin took her in her arms and carried her backstage where her mother stood waiting. The moment Kayla saw her mother, she ran towards her and hugged her solemnly.

"Mrs. Anderson, is everything alright? Kayla seemed to be in some kind of stress since morning and now as you can see, she burst into tears. I am very concerned." Mrs. Martin said sympathetically. "It's probably just stage fright." Mrs. Anderson answered quietly as she patted Kayla's hair out of her face. "She'll feel better when we get home." Joyce smiled to satisfy Mrs. Martin then walked away with Kayla in her arms. Joyce knew Kayla was expecting to see her father here, but Chris would not show up to support anything his daughter was doing. He never made any time for her. He was always busy doing other things. Of course, Kayla wasn't aware of this yet.

Back at home, tucked into bed, Kayla lay thinking. She had been waiting for Dad. Why hadn't he come when he had promised? She was so upset. He never came to pick her up from school or drop her to school. All her friends came with their Dads except her. Kayla felt tears leaping down her eyes again and fell asleep with wet weeping eyes.

Early morning on her first day of Kindergarten, Kayla was awakened out of her sleep. "I don't have time for this!" Chris said angrily. Kayla heard the door thump as her father walked out of the house, slamming it shut after him.

"I am ready, Mommy." Kayla announced as she clambered down the stairs with her backpack on her shoulders. She was so excited to meet all the new teachers and to make new friends. She was also happy because, on the first day of school, she knew both parents were requested to attend with their kids for meet and greet. She was thrilled that she would be able to ride with Dad today.

"Alright, sweetheart. Just give me ten minutes, okay? Mommy's going to book us a bus ride." Joyce answered, wiping her face and walking over to the coat rack to get her jacket with her phone inside the pocket. "We're going with Dad in the car!" Kayla exclaimed not understanding what her mother meant by the bus. "Dad has left for the office, dear. He had an important meeting to attend. You and I will find a nice ride. Come on." Joyce held out her hand for Kayla to take, who looked quite upset. "I don't want to go without Dad! I want to ride with Dad this morning!" Kayla pouted. "Kayla, honey, Dad doesn't have the time to go to school. Mommy's here. Mommy will take you. Come, sweetie, take Mommy's hand. We'll get a bus. Is that okay?" Joyce said compassionately. "No, it's not! Kayla shouted. Where's Daddy? Daddy, where are you?!"

Kayla ran all over the house. She checked her parents' bedroom. She checked the bathrooms. She checked the kitchen, but she couldn't find her father. She looked out the living room window and noticed her father car was gone. She took off her backpack and threw it in a corner. "I am not going!" Then she ran back upstairs before her mother could force her to calm down.

Six months later, Joyce stood talking to Chris in their living room. "Why don't you understand? She is noticing everything." Joyce said with uneasiness. "I don't actually care if she has!" Chris answered harshly. Both of them stood arguing obliviously while Kayla stood listening to them. She stood behind the door frame, peeking in from the side. "How can you say that? That's our daughter and she loves you!" Joyce said on the verge of tears herself.

She had seen Kayla yearn for her father's attention ever since she had been a born. She had always wanted Chris to play with her, give her time, make her laugh and make her feel as if she mattered. But Chris found one excuse after another to avoid Kayla. Sometimes it was work, at others, he was not in the mood. At bizarre times, he behaved like he didn't care at all. Joyce had initially ignored this behavior because she thought, perhaps, Chris was still a bit immature. However, with time, his attitude became too much for her to handle. He began ignoring Kayla altogether, and Joyce ended up filling that gap in Kayla's life. Now, she believed she knew the real reason for his behavior.

"Look, Chris, I get it." She started gulping down all the pain she had suffered because of him. "You don't love me anymore. I hear you. But this is our daughter.

You can't ignore her. She deserves a father. She deserves to get to know you. How can you do this to her? Why would you want to do this to her?" Joyce said while holding back tears. "She doesn't matter, Joyce. I am done with everything that's connected to you. I don't care about you or your daughter. I have a life waiting for me, outside of this trap, you call home". Chris flung his hands up in disgust.

"When we started our lives together, Joyce, you were different. You were pretty, you had ambition, and you wanted to conquer the world. The moment you had Kayla, all you think about is her. Look at yourself in the mirror. You don't take care of yourself. Our house is a mess. And it's all happening because of Kayla. I loved you. We had a life together, but you had to go and keep the baby and destroy everything. That was your choice, not mine! Now, you stick around and take care of her but don't expect me to do the same. I didn't ask you to do this to us. You managed to do it all by yourself!" Chris shook his head continuously in disbelief.

Joyce finally broke down in tears. She had decided to keep the baby when Chris had asked her to abort the child. However, she had not expected her life to fall apart because of this one decision. She had expected this child to bring joy and peace in their lives, and yet here they were. "I know it was my choice. But you don't have to punish her for it. She has done nothing to deserve it. She didn't ask to be here. Chris, she just wants her father." Joyce said desperately as the tears flowed down her cheeks.

Kayla still observing from behind the door, watched as her father sighed heavily. He pulled out his handkerchief and wiped her Mom's face then sat her down on the couch. He sat down beside her. When Joyce finally stopped crying, he spoke up again. "I am sorry, Joyce. It's too late. I am not going to change my mind. I have found my soulmate, and I don't want to live without her. Even if I'd given time to Kayla, it wouldn't change our divorce and it wouldn't change that she would have to learn to live without me anyway. I know this is hard for you. But Kayla will understand as soon as she grows up. You won't even have to explain to her. I have made up my mind, and my decision is final." Chris said firmly with his arms crossed.

Chris pulled out an envelope from his bag. Near the television stand were a couple of suitcases packed and standing in the living room. One handbag lay on the couch. He gently handed the envelope to Joyce, who didn't open it. "Goodbye, Joyce." Chris whispered, slipped the bag onto his shoulder, picked up the suitcases and began dragging them towards the door.

"Daddy, don't go! Don't go Daddy!" Kayla came running into the living room and without halting, ran to her father. She wrapped her tiny hands around his knees, holding him where he stood. "Please, don't go, Daddy." Kayla began crying as she heard Joyce sobbing behind her as she sat on the couch. Her father didn't look down at her. He was looking anywhere but at her. He looked at his watch as if he was getting late. He waited for a few minutes. "Joyce." He said, looking down at Kayla when she wouldn't let him go. "Let Daddy go, sweetheart." Joyce attempting to persuade Kayla to come over to her. "Daddy's got to go somewhere important." Joyce wiped her face. "He'll be back in the morning." "No, he won't!" Kayla screamed. "Don't go, Daddy! Daddy!"

Joyce stood up, walked to the front door, and pulled Kayla away from her father. She picked her up as Kayla cried her heart out into Joyce's shoulder. Chris didn't stay. He walked out the moment Joyce had turned away from him with Kayla in her arms. Kayla saw Chris walk out the door. She kept reaching out for him, screaming for him not to leave but Chris seemed to have turned deaf to her screams.

A year later, it was the first day of first grade. "Have a nice day, sweetheart!" Joyce said as Kayla closed the car door. Kayla glance a few cars and noticed Madison, her best friend, step out of her car. Her father stepped out as well and kissed her on the cheek before he left. She watched Madison in jealousy, run towards her.

Madison wouldn't shut up about how pleasant the ride to school had been with her dad. Kayla didn't care, but deep down, she knew she was never going to ride with her dad ever again. Not that her father had ever cared about taking her to school when they lived together. But ever since he had left, Kayla hadn't even heard his voice. He never even called.

A girl's first love is her father. That's true for every girl who has felt her father's love and care. Many unfortunate girls never get to experience this love either because they lose their father at an early age, or they are part of a broken family. Kayla's story is no different. She wants to know the excitement Madison feels when her father brings her to school.

Children, especially girls, want to show people how much their father loves them. Girls want to be their daddy's little Princess. As girls grow up, this love from their father turns into protection. Every girl feels safe and confident with her father by her side. She knows and feels the confidence that nothing bad will happen to her if she was with her father. Her dad would always be there to protect her.

After her father walked out of her life when she was five years old, Kayla lost this sense of safety and protection. She felt a void inside of her and couldn't feel as confident as Madison because she didn't have her father to count on. She felt insecure and unprepared to face the world.

CHAPTER 2

THE LOOK IN THE MIRROR

"The most beautiful thing you can wear is confidence."

~ Blake Lively

Five years later, Kayla is midway through her sixth grade year. Joyce sat in the Principal's office beside Kayla who sat clutching her book bag to her front, with her chin resting on it. "I will speak to her and I will make sure I get through this time." Joyce said sarcastically. "Kayla, dear, are you feeling alright now?" Mr. Smith, the Principal, bent forward on his desk, looked at her and asked kindly. Kayla didn't look up at him. Her gaze drilling holes in the table before her. She nodded when she heard his question but didn't look up at him.

"Sweetheart, why don't you wait for me outside?" Joyce patted Kayla's hair as she stood up uncomfortably and walked out of the Principal's office with her face towards the floor. "Ms. Joyce, we have excellent counselors on campus. I need your permission to put Kayla in a few sessions. She can use the help." Mr. Smith said to Joyce. Joyce sighed. "I don't believe she needs to see a counselor. She is just eleven years old and still trying to find herself. She hasn't been the same since her father abandoned her. I don't want to pressurize her into feeling better. She will come around as soon as she gets over it.

She's very dedicated to school however, she just doesn't socialize much. Is it anything wrong with staying to yourself?" Joyce said to Mr. Smith. "I understand how difficult it may be to acknowledge that your daughter needs therapy, but she is eleven years old, she will be an adult soon who will need to socialize in order to effectively move forward in life." Mr. Smith paused to see Joyce turn a bit angry but he continued nevertheless. "Kayla is the least confident girl in her class. She doesn't have any friends. She never participates in class. She doesn't attend social events the school organizes every year. She is particularly hesitant of the male members of her class and all of this is very unhealthy for her.

You mentioned that she hasn't filled the void left by her father's departure and, unfortunately, we can all see that. She needs to open up and talk about this with someone. If she does that with you, that's great, but if that's not going to happen, I highly recommend her speaking with the school counselor. Do you understand, Joyce?" Joyce nodded quietly. She understood why Mr. Smith was insisting on this and she knew he was absolutely right about Kayla.

Just a few weeks later, Kayla stood still looking at herself in disgust in the bedroom mirror as she got dressed for school. "I am so ugly. I am the fattest girl at school. The boys would never like me, just look at me and, all the other girls are so much prettier than I am." "Hurry up, let's go, you are going to be late to school", Joyce yelled upstairs to Kayla. Kayla, abruptly raged downstairs, swiftly passed her mother without glancing at her. Slammed the front door.

Joyce stood in the living room in astonishment as to what had Kayla in such an uproar this morning. "Kayla, are you ok sweetie?" Joyce said with concern once they were in the comfort of the car. Kayla began uncontrollably weeping. She didn't answer and continued gazing out the passenger side window. Joyce, stretched over and wiped the tears from Kayla's cheek. "Sweetheart, are you ok?" Joyce, said to Kayla softly. "I hate everything about me. I'm ugly, I'm fat, and no one likes me. No one wants to be my friend. They all laugh at me at school." Kayla, shouted at Joyce. "That's not true at all Kayla, you are very beautiful, you are amazingly smart and you rank top in your class. Just because you are uniquely different doesn't mean you are less. We are all uniquely made." Joyce, said sympathetically to Kayla.

Two years has gone by and Kayla is now, thirteen years old and in the 8th grade. She is still not the most favorite amongst her peers. Not much has changed. Her appearance is similar and she has maintained to have little to no friends. Shortly after spring break, Kayla was walking down the hall after leaving the lunch room. Kayla was just a few paces ahead when a group of girls following her burst into laughter.

Shortly after, all of Kayla's classmates began passing by her in the hallway, laughing at her. She didn't know what was going on, so she ignored it. She didn't have any friends in high school so she never spoke to anyone anyway. There was no reason to start today. Before going to the class, she decided to make a stop to put her science book back in her locker. "Hey, fatso, not so shy today, are you?" One of the boys in her class, known as the school bully pushed past her but she didn't understand what he had just said to her.

Kayla had just opened her locker when Mindy opened her locker behind her. Every locker door had a mirror attached to it for students' convenience. Kayla's eyes fell on her mirror and reflected in it she saw Mindy's locker's mirror. She was about to close her own locker and walk away when she saw Mindy's reflection laugh and high-five her friend after pointing to Kayla. She decided to see what Mindy was pointing at exactly and froze where she stood. Her pants had torn on the rear side and her underpants and butt cheeks were visible to the whole school!

Kayla was more than embarrassed. Kayla had tears in her eyes when she saw Mindy laughing at her. She pulled a book out of the locker, covered her rear with it and attempted to make her way to the girls room as fast as she could. Before she had taken a couple of steps more, Mindy and her friends blocked her way to the girls' room and deliberately dragged her inside the classroom. The moment they let go, she was about to run out when Will entered the classroom. He had been her crush for the past three years but she could never tell him. If she walked by him outside, he too would see the tear in her pants. Confused and worried, Kayla sat down quickly.

The moment class ended, she waited for everyone to leave. Nevertheless, everyone sat laughing and pointing at her. And then the worst thing happened. She heard multiple cell phone alerts. At the same time, her phone buzzed too. Everyone in class pulled their cell phones out instantly. She looked at the video she had just received. The video was her walking in the hallway at school with her underwear and butt cheeks exposed. Kayla's face turned red and her eyes watered up. She looked up and saw Will staring at the video in his phone, laughing with the rest of the class. He looked at her smirking then left the classroom. Almost everyone left the classroom looking and laughing at their phones.

The moment everyone was gone, Kayla sprinted in the direction of the girls' room. When she entered the restroom it was empty. She froze at the mirrors in front of her. She was a stout girl, not any taller than five feet. She had round shoulders, a round face and due to her excessive weight, she looked like a butterball. Her brown hairs were thick like wool and her black eyes were barely visible on her big round face. She looked at her reflection in distaste. She looked awful and ugly. Before she could control them, thick tears ran down her eyes. She couldn't wait for this day to be over.

Later that evening Kayla arrived home. "How was your day dear?" Joyce said as Kayla walked through the front door. "It was awful, the worst day of my life." Kayla answered her mother and stormed upstairs.

After that day, Kayla asked her mother to write a sick note for her so she could get three days of peace. She was sure after this time her video would be long forgotten. Joyce didn't question it because it was not the first time Kayla had asked her to do something like this. There had been occasions when Kayla had requested her write sick notes for even a full week. Joyce knew something was wrong with Kayla but she also knew Kayla wouldn't tell her if she asked. She was also a bit afraid to ask. She knew how sensitive Kayla was about her weight. She didn't want to upset her more by talking about it. She just wished she could give her daughter the kind of confidence she needed.

Joyce knew losing her father was the calamity that had shattered Kayla's confidence and self-esteem. She had tried her absolute best to prepare her for life but she couldn't replace the love and confidence Kayla could have had if her father was active in her life.

After three days of leave and the weekend, Kayla must return to school finally. On Sunday evening before turning in, Kayla stood in front of the mirror scrutinizing every detail about her appearance. It was as if she didn't like anything about herself. She wondered if she were slimmer, she would look better. She didn't really have any boobs or a butt. Her lips were too thin. She needed to pluck her brows and she didn't even like her hair. She went to bed scared of the morning.

When the sun raised in the morning, Kayla was awakened by her mother. "Get up Kayla, you overslept. You will be late if you don't hurry." Joyce said with urgency. As she sluggishly forced herself out of bed, she could only think about what her first day back to school would be like after her most embarrassing moment of her life. Complete silence the entire car ride to school. Kayla quietly departed her mother's car. "Have a great day sweetheart." Joyce smiling at her. Kayla didn't reply. She stood on the sidewalk momentarily with a blank stare, as she watched all the other kids cheerfully enter the school.

Finally, she built enough courage and began walking towards the school entrance front door. As Kayla, walked down the hallway and passed many of her peers no one seemed to have noticed her. Just as she hoped for her embarrassing moment was no longer the topic and laughing matter of the school. She took a deep breath, indicating a sigh of relief as she proceeded to her first class.

We put so much propaganda in people's appearances, that we overlook their entire personality. The same thing happened to Kayla in her early teenage years. She struggled with obesity in middle school and didn't come out on the brighter end of things when she tried to overcome her insecurities. Kayla's story isn't new to many teenagers as they face bullying at school every single day, either because they're not perfectly shaped, they're not tall enough or they're not popular enough.

Girls who have experienced their father's company are more likely to be confident about how they look, because the first man in their life, demonstrated unconditional love. The ones who never get to know what that's like occasionally end up like Kayla, unconfident and fragile on the inside.

CHAPTER 3

THE SECRETS KEPT

You never know what someone is dealing with behind closed doors. You only know what you see or what you think you see.

~ Mackenzie Phillips

As several years went by, Kayla had transformed into a beautiful young lady during her senior year of high school after suffering a not-so-happy middle school term. She had lost a tremendous amount of weight, dressed well and began to gain confidence in her appearance. She also realized how people had altered the way they interacted with her, which was totally contradictory of her experience in middle school. Kayla was definitely more sociable now than ever before and was semi-popular amongst her classmates. She was the team Captain of her cheer squad and voluntarily participated in school events.

At the beginning of her senior year a gentleman by

the name of Scott Russell introduced himself to her in the hallway during brief passing. Scott was several years older than Kayla and had a career as a professional business man. He also worked part-time as a substitute teacher at the high school she attended. Scott and Kayla dated privately for one year due to her being underage and still in high school. She immediately became infatuated with him, captivated by his smooth talk and fell in love with his charm. Kayla thought with a gentle smile on her face, "Someone finally loves me for who I am".

Just as Kayla graduated and soon after turning eighteen, Scott proposed to her. "Yes! Yes! Yes!" Kayla replied happily to the man who knelt before her with the beautiful diamond ring in his hand. Kayla didn't think twice before saying yes. Love like his, she thought she would never find it again. Scott flattered her with money and extravagant gifts, expressed love and thoughtfulness that she had never experienced. The type of love she desperately desired from her father.

Scott had no children and was never married. He had thick, black curly hair that stood up on his head like a cotton ball. He had big brown eyes and a smile that could make Kayla feel butterflies in her stomach, even after one year of dating. Scott appeared to be the perfect gentleman. There was no way Kayla was going to allow a man like this to pass her by.

Joyce blessed her daughter a happy new life with all of her heart. She was so happy to see Kayla joyful but she was also concerned about her at the same time. Kayla was only eighteen years old at this time. Joyce knew she was too young and immature to know if she was making the right decision but it was her choice to make. Joyce contemplated but couldn't dare interfere with her decision.

One year later on her wedding day, Kayla was the happiest woman on earth. She had finally felt that she was worthy of love and one that will last forever. The wedding was everything she dreamed. She wore a long white ball gown with lots of flounce, bustle and sparkle fit for a princess. Hair pinned up in a bun with fancy curls and a crystal tiara to complete her fairytale look. She arrived on a horse drawn carriage. Guests were enchanted with breathtaking decorations blooming archways, vintage candelabras, crystal chandeliers, fairy light filled mason jars to create a magical fairy tale wedding.

"Kayla, wow your wedding is very beautiful. I am so happy for you. You are very fortunate to have found a man like Scott." Theresa, a friend of Scott said excitingly to Kayla. Shortly after and unexpectedly, Kayla overheard a group of young women at a nearby table chattering. She thinks she is all that because she married Scott. I don't see what he sees in her. She is not attractive and dresses like an old lady. He could've chosen a much prettier and popular young lady to marry. Kayla prancing by them in her beautiful gown, looked over at the young ladies gossiping and waved at them. While many were sincerely happy for Kayla there were surprisingly quite a few envious of her as well. They were jealous of the lifestyle she had gained. Kayla, was the first of her peers to marry a successful businessman. Even her closest friends began to envy her.

After everyone had danced their hearts out and the evening came to an end, Kayla and Scott made an astonishing grand exit. Guests quickly lined outside to create an illuminate pathway for them to walk through. Sparkles crackled and guests cheered. Kayla suddenly caught a glance of the all-white, horse drawn Cinderella carriage. She beamed at Scott, clutched his hand. They both climbed delightfully unto the carriage and Kayla fell lightly into the comfort of Scott's arms. "Baby, you're the best thing that happened to me!" Kayla whispered in Scott's ear, while admiring the rustic beauty as they traveled along charming pathways. Kayla was happier than ever to be his wife. Scott turned towards her and gazed into her eyes. "You too." He smiled. Kayla blushed.

The next morning dawned with joy, Kayla woke up early and made breakfast for Scott, while he was in the bathroom preparing for work. Everything was exactly as he liked it. Kayla stood waiting for him at the kitchen counter in her sexy lingerie. He looked amazing and smelled great, she admired him as he entered into the kitchen. They ate breakfast together then Kayla went in for her shower. When Kayla came out, Scott was sitting on the bed waiting with anticipation for her with an envelope in his hand.

"What's this?" Kayla asked inquisitively. She was quite

excited inside. This could be tickets to their honeymoon. She stood waiting in eagerness. "Take a look." He handed her the envelope. Inside the envelope, Kayla found an offer letter for a job in another state. "When did you apply?" Kayla questioned with concern. "Right before the wedding. I received the letter yesterday and I wanted to surprise you. We were so busy with the wedding on yesterday that we didn't have time to discuss it. But I know we're going to have a great life there." Scott said, kissed her on the forehead and walked away taking the letter from her.

"Scott, but it says you have to be there by next month." Kayla whined. "Yeah, isn't it great?" Scott replied with excitement. "It's too fast. Scott, I've lived here all my life and as long as I have known you, so have you. How will we adjust?" Kayla said sadly. "We will make it work. It's a great paying job. We wouldn't have to worry about anything. Don't worry about the details." Scott answered her confidently. "But Scott, my mom's here." Kayla insisted. Scott didn't have anyone in his family here. His parents had passed away when he was five years old, from a tragic car accident. He had been raised by relatives who were no longer part of his life after he became an adult. But Kayla had her mom in this state and she had a life that she wasn't very willing to leave behind.

"I'm not asking, Kayla. We are leaving soon, so be ready to go." Scott said demandingly then walked out of the house slamming the front door when she opened her mouth to answer.

Time flew by, a month had passed since they discussed Scott accepting a job position in another state. The day prior to departure Scott returned home early from work. Kayla was expected to have packed their belongings by the time he got off work as they had to travel in the morning. When Scott entered the bedroom, Kayla was sitting somberly on the bed with her head down. Several empty suitcase were lying on the floor next to her. She hadn't packed anything. She was uncomfortable with the fact of leaving her mother behind.

"You, bitch!" Kayla fell on the carpeted floor of their bedroom. Scott had slapped her right across the face so hard, she had fallen right off the bed. Tears escaped her eyes as pain engulfed her. Before she could catch her breath, Scott pulled her back to her feet by her hair. "Look into my eyes when I talk to you!" He scolded her, holding her face right up close to his. "Now, what's the rule in my house?" He asked aggressively. "That—that I do as I am told." Kayla stuttered. Scott let go of her hair. "Good, now go do as you were told! Have our clothes packed in an hour."

"I'm going out." Scott said demandingly as he walked out the bedroom leaving Kayla home alone, quite miserable, and packing clothes. The moment, Scott left, Kayla burst into tears. It had been only one year since they got married. Scott didn't seem like the same man she had married. He was beginning to be a totally different person. He was rude. He called her horrible names. He was disrespectful and didn't value her.

A few days later, they arrived at their new home in their new town. Scott was expected to start work in just a few days. Since their marriage, he had forbidden her to take on any kind of job. She was supposed to be a stay-at-home wife and maintain his home while he went outside to 'earn their bread and butter' as he put it. A few weeks later he struck her again. When Kayla tried to fight back, he beat her down into a pulp. Kayla had been hospitalized for a week. He told the doctors, she had been in an accident and ever since then, he had petrified her to deal with his outbursts of anger if she didn't want to be beaten down again.

Kayla had been dealing with his abuse and torture for the past year. She hadn't mentioned a word about it to her mother who thought she was living a happy and content life with her husband. Joyce had no clue the hell Kayla had been living in. Furthermore, Kayla had stayed silent because a month ago, she had learned she was pregnant. She wasn't showing yet and hadn't told Scott as she was waiting for the perfect time to tell him.

She revealed the baby to Scott in the fourth month of her pregnancy. At first, he had tried to talk her out of having the child. He had attempted to convince her to have an abortion. But Kayla just couldn't and wouldn't dare do that. She had a feeling her baby was going to change her life. Her baby was going to fill that void for love she had been chasing all her life. She had unsympathetically denied Scott's request to abort the child. Consequently,

My Tears Are in His Hands

he stopped harassing her about it. She felt he just wasn't ready to be a father and he would come around once he held the child in his arms.

Unpredictably, in her last month of pregnancy, he asked her to visit her mother so she could help out with the baby after delivery. Hesitantly, Kayla contemplated. She was concerned about traveling alone in her last month of pregnancy. "Scott, what if I go into labor early?" Kayla said fearfully. "Everything will be just fine babe and I will be there before the baby arrives." Scott promised.

Shortly after, Kayla arrived back at her hometown with her mother. "Where is Scott?" Joyce asked with concern. "Oh, he will be here soon. He had to attend to a few business affairs before leaving." Kayla replied with confidence.

"Congratulations!" Joyce hugged Kayla enthusiastically when she met her at the hospital after delivery. Kayla had just become a mother to a beautiful precious little girl, named Marcella. "Thanks, Mom. Can you believe it? You're a grandmother!" Kayla said is disbelief. Kayla was happier than she had ever felt, holding her little baby in her hand. She was the most precious thing that had ever happened to her.

"Any news?" said Kayla. Since she had gone into labor, Joyce had been attempting to reach Scott by phone. But he hadn't answered any of her calls. Joyce shook her head in disbelief. Trying to understand why Scott wasn't here with his wife and new baby girl. And why he hadn't answered any of her calls. Kayla also called Scott several times when they got back home from the hospital but he still didn't answer.

Joyce sorted through the mail she had missed in the two days they had spent at the hospital. "Kayla, it's from Scott." Joyce handed her an envelope not really looking at it, as she checked the bills. Kayla took the envelope and tore it open. She placed the baby on the couch so she could pull out the papers inside. The moment she had wished she had never opened the envelope. It was a divorce papers from Scott.

Many women stay in abusive marriages despite having the most disturbing time in their lives. Women who feel they would never find a partner who could love them for real, settle for ungrateful and abusive partners who don't deserve them. Kayla was no different and she was suffering and confused because she had never felt what it was like to be truly loved by a man.

She dreamed of a perfect wedding day, beautifully family and living happily ever after just as every other woman. She definitely never would have desired to be divorced and a single mother, raising her child on her own. Remorsefully, she knew first-hand the void that an absent father would have on her child.

CHAPTER 4

THE BATTLES OF LIFE

"Above all, be the heroine of your life. Not the victim."

~ Nora Ephron

The divorce papers came as a blow to Kayla, it snatched the ground from underneath her feet and crumbled the last bits of the illusion of marriage that she had created for herself. It came as a disappointment, but not a surprise. Because she didn't want to acknowledge it, but deep down, she had expected it. She knew that the way Scott had been treating her that he no longer loved her.

They say history repeats itself, and from the moment she had gotten pregnant in an unhappy marriage, there had been a nagging voice that she had silenced in her mind. As her childhood life flashed before her, she realized this is what had happened to her mother. The very same reason she had hidden her pregnancy from her soon to be ex-husband was not only the fact that she didn't know if he was ready for a child, but a big part of it was fear of out-right rejection. The abandonment that she had faced at the hands of her own father who had never loved her. What a terrible feeling to acknowledge that your daughter will experience the same void of an absent father just like her mother.

She sat at the kitchen table slowly with the divorce papers in her hand coming to terms with what had happened. The sound of her precious child crying in the background and her mother trying to calm the baby down, she couldn't help but admit to herself that she was somewhat calmed. She was thankful that her child would have a clean slate from the start and would not have to face the feeling of being rejected by her father. She was also relieved that her child wouldn't have to face her mother being abused and disrespected by a father who doesn't love either of them. Her hands trembled a little while sitting at the kitchen table. While her erratically beating heart was calming down, she quickly realized the main issues in all of this.

Although it was a decision she rather not have had to make, it actuality she knew it was for the best for her and her daughter. To finally begin her life from a fresh start, she would have to go through the tedious procedures of a typical divorce with Scott before she could be at peace with her child. Someone who she thought had loved her as much as she loved him. All these thoughts and realizations made Kayla burst into tears. Her heart was heavy, confused, and shattered. For the first time in a long time, Kayla allowed herself to let out her emotions. She allowed herself to cry her heart out. She wailed because she felt another piece of her barely tethered heart chip away. Kayla felt her mother's comforting hands on her shoulders, she left all thoughts of keeping herself composed and leaned into her mother's touch as she cried even more.

The next week went by hastily. Kayla was slowly coming to terms with the fact that the love of her life had left her. Not only that, but realized he had never loved her in the first place. Then what had she been to him this whole time? Kayla wondered.

The divorce papers sat on the kitchen counter for another full week. Kayla refused to look at them. Instead, she busied herself with tending to the care and needs of Marcella. Taking care of Marcella eased her worries, if only temporarily. She knew when Marcella was hungry, when her diaper was full, and when she felt sick. It was as if she was connected to her in a way she had never been connected to another. As she breastfed Marcella she reminisced the day she had chosen her name. Marcella, It means warlike. Kayla smiled at her little angel who was fast asleep in her arms. "She comes to me when I am facing the most terrible battles of life, naming her so, will strengthen her to fight back as I never could." Kayla said with reassurance. Her voice cracked at the end and her mother wiped the lone tear that escaped her.

She gathered the divorce papers and held them not long afterward. As she twirled the pen in her hand and looked at the space she was supposed to pen her signature, she felt both relief and the impending doom that would be facing Scott again in the courtroom. Scott never wanted a child so, I'm quite sure he will not battle me for Marcella, Kayla thought. Marcella would be rejected like she had been so long ago by her own father. She put on her glasses and read the terms of the divorce petition 'the marriage existing between the Parties is irretrievably broken'.

But she felt a strange unease when she recalled it was Scott who had filed for divorce on those grounds in the first place. She was the one who had bent herself backward during their marriage. She was the one who gave up everything for him. She was the one who suffered verbal, physical and mental abuse from him. Yet, in the end, he was always the one who manipulated there marital problems to make everything seem to be her fault. She had ended up being called disobedient, disrespectful, nagging, and useless as a wife. She took a deep breath and signed the papers.

One month after Marcella was born, Kayla was getting dressed, and she was pulling down her shirt when she felt a slight bump as she slid the blouse down. At first, she brushed it off, but then she shook her head and pulled her shirt back off to look at herself closely in the mirror. She pulled down her bra strap and lifted her arm up. She noticed a round bulge right near her armpit. She cautiously placed her fingers on the lump to examine it. The mass felt like a rock with rigid edges. She gulped and pulled the strap back up. It was probably nothing, right? She assured herself and continued getting dressed. She was getting ready to travel back to her ex-husbands home as they prepared for divorce court the next morning.

Later that evening Kayla had returned to her previous home with only a few belongings. As Scott opened the entrance door of his home, he greeted her with a disgusting look on his face. "Come in Kayla," Scott said with aggravation. Kayla didn't respond but walked in carelessly. She didn't understand why Scott was being so rude to her, his wife and the mother of his child. He hadn't seen her in a month. Scott kept their home and all of their belongings. At that point, she realized she didn't want anything from Scott anymore, not even the items in the house.

Scott told her to make herself comfortable on the couch. He then proceeded to the back of the home, went into his bedroom and closed the door.

The remaining evening went by in silence. As Kayla, laid on the couch her mind wandered. Scott hadn't asked about Marcella. He didn't even ask to see a picture of her. It hadn't been long, but it had felt like an eternity since Kayla was in the home. Her eyes teared up and she eventually drifted herself to sleep.

The next morning they arrived at the courthouse. "Mr. & Mrs. Russell please enter the courtroom," the judge said as they are escorted in the courtroom by the bailiff. They quietly took their seats on opposing sides of the long mahogany table, with their lawyers on each side. "Court is now in session." The judge announced. "Please present your case!" The judge stated. "Your Honor, My client

Scott Russell has filed for Dissolution of Marriage. He has deemed the marriage existing between the Parties are irretrievably broken." Scott's lawyer further announced, "Mr. Scott waive his rights to joint custody and wants no duty in raising their daughter Marcella."

Scott avoided eye contact with Kayla all together as he stared at the spot on the wall while his lawyer narrated how he didn't want any responsibility with raising Marcella.

Kayla laughed internally. She crossed her arms. "So you're just going to abandon your own daughter? You are going to completely walk out of her life? Where is your role as her father? You are pitiful, just pitiful," Kayla said with disgust. Scott's lawyer intervened, but it was too late. Kayla's lawyer had taken her lead and defended her case.

ORDERED AND ADJUDGED

- The marriage between the parties Scott Russell and Kayla Russell is dissolved and the parties are restored to the status of being single.
- The wife name has been restored to Kayla Anderson.
- Full custody of child, Marcella Russell has been granted to the mother, Kayla Russell.
- Visitation Rights of child, Marcella Russell has been granted to the father, Scott Russell.
- The father Scott Russell has been ordered to pay child support for the child, Marcella Russell in the amount of six hundred and seventy five dollars.

In the end, the divorce was finalized and Kayla walked away with full custody of her daughter and a reasonable amount of child support. Scott received visitation rights with no other obligation to care for his daughter.

When Kayla returned home the next day to her daughter and mother, she hugged her mother and cried again. The feeling of loss was still there. And it felt like it would stay there for a while. While they were hugging she felt a strong irritating itch under her armpit and jerked back immediately. "Is everything okay, love?" Joyce asked with concern. Her face was grimacing and tears filling her eyes. "Yes, mom. I'll be back, I just have to use the bathroom, okay?" Kayla said doubtfully.

She went into the bathroom, lifted her blouse, and raised her arm in the air. Closely observing in the mirror she noticed a substantial change in the appearance of the hard rocky lump under her armpit. Redness. Pain. Skin flaking like orange peels, Kayla began to be concerned. She immediately knew it was time to make an appointment.

Three days later Kayla was at her doctor's office for a checkup. She decided to have it evaluated by a physician who had ordered her a biopsy. Marcella was weening now, as she had stopped breast feeding once she discovered a lump in her breast several days ago. She was anxious for the procedure however, fearing the results. Outside the procedure room, Joyce stood waiting patiently for her with Marcella in her hands. Kayla was frantically terrified and without Joyce by her side she would never have come alone.

A couple days later, Kayla accompanied by Joyce and Marcella returned to the doctor's office. Unfortunately, the doctor didn't have very good news. "Kayla, my dear I am very sorry to inform you that your pathology test revealed a malignant tumor in your right breast." The doctor said sympathetically. The doctor advised Kayla to stay calm as there are many successful treatment options. There were many women who were living healthy and happy lives after they had been cured of breast cancer. You most definitely could be one of those women with proper treatment. Kayla was devastated by this news. She was already overwhelmed by her circumstances. She was recently divorced, trying to figure out how to get her life together for herself and her daughter, and now this. She has to battle one of the most leading fears of a woman, breast cancer!

Kayla took her doctors recommendations and promptly began chemotherapy. Chemotherapy was suggested by her doctor to attempt to control the cancer and decrease any symptoms associated with the disease. Shortly, after beginning treatment Kayla started having terrible side effects. She began to be overly depressed as she experienced significant hair loss, nausea, vomiting, and fatigue. Kayla once again became self-conscious about her appearance. She was losing herself day by day. The thoughts of ever finding love again now seemed hopeless. She went through chemotherapy and hormone therapy and finally after one year of battling she was cancer-free.

CHAPTER 5

THE BREAKING POINT

"Everyone has a breaking point no matter, how strong they are".

- Lisa Gupta

Seven months after she was cleared of all symptoms of breast cancer, she found herself watching her daughter's first steps. "Kayla!" Her mother's voice snapped her out of her daydream. She turned her gaze from the garden outside the window she was standing in front of to her mother who was excitedly motioning with her hand behind her. "Yes?" Kayla said and cleared her throat. "Come here, Kayla. You have to see this! It's Marcella!" Joyce exclaimed with excitement.

Kayla blinked a few times and followed her mother out into the living room where Marcella was on her knees amidst a plethora of toys on the floor. Kayla passed a confused gaze to her mother and then looked back at her daughter who simply wobbled a bit and stood on both feet, taking a few steps forward before falling back down. "Marcella, come to grandma! Come here, sweetie!" Joyce called out as she sat down on the floor to get on the child's level.

Kayla watched as her daughter stood up and smiled wide at Joyce. Seeing Marcella smile filled Kayla up with the kind of joy she had never known before. But strangely, as Marcella wobbled her way and took her little baby steps while cooing and giggling right into her grandmother's arms. Kayla's heart started feeling heavier, she forced a smile on her face as she picked up her lovely child and twirled her in her arms. She was truly so happy to see this milestone in her child's life. But then why was her heart heavy and her mind gloomy? "Kayla, you haven't been yourself lately at all. Tell me, love. Tell me what's wrong." Joyce stated as she placed a hand on Kayla's shoulder. "I don't know, mom. I feel like everything in my life has gone wrong. I never received the love and attention from my father, my husband divorced me, I am a single mother and cancer tried to take my life. What is it to be happy for?" Kayla answered, feeling hollow." "There is a lot to be happy for, darling." Joyce's face contorted.

Kayla found herself to be immersed in major depressive episodes frequently. She had experience depression and loneliness symptoms before in her earlier school age years but they were never this tense. She spent most of her days doing absolutely nothing and counting down the hours to return to bed. Even her daughter wasn't giving her the joy she once had. Kayla lately was leaving Marcella's care to her mother as she dragged herself in and out of bed each day. Her battles of life have pushed her to a breaking point that she can no longer cope with her stress on her own.

"You're depressed, aren't you? It's okay to be broken but don't stay there long." Joyce replied with concern. Kayla nodded. "Do you want to go talk to the doctor tomorrow?" Joyce asked. Her voice was calm, soothing yet cautious. "No, mom. Not just yet." Kayla shook her head. "I just need some time. I'll be okay."

As she lay in bed that night, she took deep breaths to ease the heaviness in her chest. The only thing that resulted from it were flashbacks from her younger years and all the times she had opened up her heart and been vulnerable.

From here as a little girl openly asking, even begging, for her father's affections to her spreading herself thin to make her marriage work. It seemed like no matter how hard she tried it was never enough. That she was never adequate and she realized how much of this had damaged her on the inside. Kayla was aware of her depression and mindful that she was still harboring on things from her childhood. At this phase in life, she had reached her breaking point. She realized it was something she needed to get control of and seek help soon. As she continued to lay fidgety in bed, her mind persistently recalled her tragic experiences in life. She tossed and turned in bed for the rest of the night.

Over the next few weeks, Kayla tried to lose herself with work around the house. She started spending more time with Marcella and daily activities. But nothing seemed to fill the void. Instead, she noticed her sleep getting more restless and her weight dropping even more. She was being consumed by depression and losing herself by the minute.

One day her mother decided to drag her out of the house to go to the nearby playground with Marcella. "Mom, you can take Marcella and go." She protested weakly. "Absolutely not." Joyce shook her head. "You've been holed up at home for more than enough. All you do is housework and lay in your bed." In the end, Kayla cleaned up and joined them. Once they reached the playground, Joyce took Marcella to play, leaving Kayla alone on the bench to think. Being outside was refreshing, Kayla realized. She breathed in the fresh air instead of the stale air in her bedroom where she was hibernating all day.

Her mind and heart were still gloomy but she felt slightly better. She was deep into her thoughts and didn't realize someone had occupied the space next to her on the bench. "Hello." The stranger greeted her, causing Kayla to snap out of her deep thoughts. She turned her head to see a beautiful older woman who looked to be in her forties sitting next to her. "Hello." Kayla smiled and responded before turning back to search for her mother and daughter. She spotted Marcella on a swing with Joyce pushing her lightly.

When she sat back she noticed the lady holding a little brown leathered book in her hand calmly reading it. "May I ask what book that is?" Kayla asked, hesitantly. "Sorry to disturb you." "You aren't disturbing me, dear. Why, this is the book of God. His words give me comfort and always have." The woman responded. "Oh my, you haven't really been in touch with Him. Have you?" Kayla flushed. It was true, she had no relationship with God. But she didn't have it in her to explain that to a total stranger. "Sorry." The lady's smile faltered. "I didn't mean to make you feel bad." "It's fine." Kayla nodded her head. "Does it help?" "It does." The lady replied. "Tell you what, you can have this." "Your book?" Kayla was surprised. "I couldn't." "Take it. I have a new copy at home." The lady shook her head. "I hope He guides you the way He did me."

Shortly after they returned home, Kayla kept holding the book in her hands. She had reached her breaking point and was in desperate need of help and comfort. She was no longer going to allow depression to get the best of her. Kayla didn't dare open it until after everyone had gone to sleep. And when she did, she found herself captivated by each and every word. The further she read the more her worries seemed too insignificant to waste tears over. It was the first step, and a small one, but she genuinely felt hope in the word of God.

CHAPTER 6

THE WORKMANSHIP OF GOD

For we are His workmanship [His own master work, a work of art], created in Christ Jesus [reborn from above-spiritually transformed, renewed, ready to be used] for good works, which God prepared [for us] beforehand [taking paths which He set], so that we would walk in them [living the good life which He prearranged and made ready for us].

- Ephesians 2:10 | AMP

As it turned out, Kayla realized that God was the only one who had truly been by her side this whole time. Starting from when she was a little girl, God had protected her in His own way and the more she delved into His words, the more she became increasingly reassured of this fact.

Her routine changed and she started waking up early to start her day with His word. After cleaning up and feeding Marcella, she would sit on the porch with her Holy Bible and watch her daughter play as she immersed herself into the wisdom and comfort given to her by the word of the Lord. Her mother noticed this. "What are you reading dear?" Joyce asked as she made her way next to Kayla on the porch swing, steaming mug of coffee in hand. Kayla simply hummed and lifted the book a little, as she continued to read it. Joyce nodded. She was glad Kayla was reading. She had always been an avid reader when she was a child but her habit had fallen off when real life obstacles started hitting her with full force.

Seeing Kayla not only reading but reading something that would strengthen her relationship with God was comforting to Joyce. Even though she had never been a very religious woman herself, she had taken Kayla to church once a month through her childhood. "Mom." Kayla turned to Joyce. Joyce nodded, motioning for her to continue. "I want to... understand the word of God better. I want us to start attending church regularly. I want Marcella to grow up being in church." From that day on, Kayla would dress Marcella for church every Sunday and they would attend worship service. Some days Joyce would not go with them, and Kayla would take her daughter by herself.

Listening to God's words and what He intended to teach humans filled her with a sense of calmness and tranquility. Mostly, Kayla would go with Marcella, attend church and return home. The other people at church would socialize and talk to each other but since Kayla didn't know anyone, she kept to herself. It worked out for her because she didn't go there to make friends, she went there to become closer to God.

During her fifth visit, when everyone dispersed and started going their ways, someone tapped Kayla on the shoulder as she made her way to the parking lot with Marcella in her stroller. She turned around and came eye to eye with the same woman who had given her the first copy of the Holy Bible and that had started her on her spiritual journey.

"Hello." Kayla smiled, which was reciprocated by the woman. "Hey. I didn't catch your name the other day? It's really nice seeing you here, sweetheart." The woman said. "Oh. I'm Kayla." Kayla answered. "And you?" "You can call me Irene." the woman replied, tucking her hair behind her ears. "Kayla, I came here to ask if you wanted to join me and some others for lunch today? We would love to have you with us." Irene asked. Kayla was a bit hesitant. She later supposed that it must be because she had been alone all those years. She never made any real friendships and her husband betrayed her in the worst ways possible. But she imagined the time she will spend this afternoon with Irene and her two friends would be something she would cherish. So, she agreed to join them.

Irene's friends were Linda and Tracey. Linda was a mother of three in her early thirties and Tracey was closer to Kayla's age, only a few years older. They had gone to the bakery near their church and ordered tea with snacks. Kayla took a slice of coffee cake with her milk tea. They sat down near the window and chatted the rest of the afternoon. By that, it means Kayla was mostly quiet and the other three made conversation, including her in it always.

"Lucas gets on my nerves." Linda rolled her eyes as she took a slurp of her tea. "He's testing my patience for real. God help me if I don't kick him out of the house by next week." Linda seemed annoyed but her tone was light-hearted, it was obvious that Lucas was someone she adored. Before she could ask who it was, Tracey spoke up. "Oh, come on," Tracey said. "He's going through early high school. It's a tough time! Let him adjust." "Oh. I know, I know." Linda waved it away. "It's just that he's always snapping about one thing or the other and I'm always stressed especially with Jonathan's work issues."

"How's Jonathan's job going? Wasn't his company letting people go?" Irene leaned forward in concern. "Yeah but hopefully not Jonathan. You know how he's helped them so much. But the worry is still there." Linda sighed and turned to Kayla. "What does your husband do, Kayla?" Kayla fell quiet as the gaze of the three women fell upon her. They waited patiently for an answer as Kayla's heart started beating a bit faster. "Oh. Um." Kayla cleared her throat, nervously. "I'm divorced. I got divorced more than a year ago. I live with my mother and Marcella in our own home." "Oh. I'm so sorry." Linda began, her kind face apologetic. "I didn't know, I didn't mean to be intrusive." "It's okay." Kayla shook her head. "I'm much better now. I promise."

"Well, you seem like a good person, Kayla," Tracey

spoke. "He must have done something big for you to leave him." "Actually, he left me," Kayla replied, smiling a little. "But I'm glad he did." The three women blinked at her, speechlessly. They seemed to want to ask more but were hesitating. So, Kayla decided to tell them. Were they meeting for the first time? Yes. But she felt safe with them and truly thought they would understand her situation. After she was done narrating her story, she noted that Irene and Linda had tears in their eyes and Tracey was sniffling. She was surprised. "Oh, Kayla." Tracey sniffled. "Get up, please." Kayla got up and Tracey enveloped her into a hug. She wasn't used to this. She wasn't used to being loved unconditionally and accepted with all her weight and baggage.

It might be a normal hug for someone else, but for her, it carried the meaning of acceptance and true care. So she leaned in and hugged Tracey back, her own eyes stinging with tears. But these were tears of joy. Once they were done, they both sat back in their seats. "Well, it's decided. Kayla is having lunch with us every Sunday now." Linda announced. "Thank you." Kayla smiled in gratitude. "For having me, despite me having rough edges." "Rough edges?" Irene exclaimed in shock. "Sweetheart, you are a miracle of God. God's masterpiece." "Irene's right. Don't say things like that. People would crumble if they went through what you've been through but here you are standing tall and strong." Tracey reassured her. A miracle of God. God's masterpiece. God is your creator and you are His workmanship, His masterwork. He knows everything about you. He took delicate time creating you for His purpose. He knows the troubles you would face and what you will become before you have actually become it.

Over the next few days, Kayla thought about this. All those years, she had felt like an outcast, a reject, and a pariah. Someone who had been exiled from God's love. She had always felt like she was unworthy and undeserving of love and warmth and was destined to live her life cold and miserable. Always having to yearn for acceptance. But Kayla recalled what had been told to her in church once before when she was younger. 'God gives his hardest battles to His greatest soldiers.'

As soon as she came to this realization, her perspective on everything changed. She no longer viewed herself as a reject but as a precious child of God. Someone whom God loved and cherished. Someone who had gone through God's tests and come out stronger. She realized that she was a work in progress and when her Father looked at her all He sees is magnificence and greatness. From that day on a big weight got lifted from her shoulders.

Finally Kayla reached this point after freeing herself from the expectations and needs to be loved by another man. Be it her father or her husband, she no longer craved their love and affections. Because she realized that the only one she truly needed was God. He would be the one to be her strength no matter what she goes through.

CHAPTER 7

THE WAIT WILL BE GREAT

But those who wait for the Lord [who expect, look for, and hope in Him] will gain new strength and renew their power; They will lift up their wings [and rise up close to God] like eagles [rising toward the sun]; They will run and not become weary, they will walk and not grow tired.

~ Isaiah 40:31 | AMP

As a few years passed, Kayla started feeling more and more confident within herself. The old timid girl who would stumble over her own words in fear that she would offend someone, who would shrink into herself as to not take up too much space and would start apologizing for things that were not even her fault wasn't completely gone. But Kayla had started walking taller, bolder and less apologetically, and it showed.

Kayla and her mother were shopping for groceries while pushing Marcella in a stroller, Kayla's elbow bumped with a stockperson, who ended up dropping the several boxes of snacks he was balancing. "I'm so sorry." She gasped apologetically while her inside tensed a little. "Let me pick that up with you." "It's no problem, Miss." The stockman responded with a small smile as they both ended up picking up the fallen boxes.

Once the stockperson had left, Kayla started pushing the stroller ahead. A few seconds in and she noticed her mother's absence by her side. She turned around and questioningly gazed at her mother who was still standing a few feet behind with a small smile on her face. "What is it?" Kayla asked, mind filled with confusion. "You've gained confidence within yourself." Joyce chuckled. "What?" Kayla laughed a bit, turning around to face her. "Nothing, oh nothing." Joyce shook her head. "Just not that long ago you would have reacted much differently to what just happened. Nothing big. Just making an observation."

Joyce caught up with her after saying that and continued walking. Kayla followed her and soon they fell back into their previous routine of marking things off the grocery list. It wasn't until they were home arranging the groceries in the kitchen when Kayla thought again about her mother's words. She recalled every incident she could remember when she had accidentally bumped into the stockperson. She used to be the kind of person who excessively apologized for the smallest things, it was almost as if she had been apologizing for simply existing. Suddenly, it dawned on her what her mother had meant. She had gained self-confidence. She was maturing out of her self-doubt and walking towards a path of self-assuredness.

The next morning, Kayla sat in front of her laptop and started writing her daily tasks, while also searching for job opportunities. Since the divorce, it was difficult to find work considering she had never been employed as she married immediately after high school, been unemployed for the entirety of her marriage and missed out on many employment and training opportunities.

Typing away her usual tasks, an idea popped into her head. She closed the tab she was working on and quickly opened the other tab, typing in the search bar for options on how to get started on getting a license to become a real estate agent. She came across an online course to become a licensed real estate agent in only 6 months. Kayla with excitement, discussed the course with her mother, Joyce. However, Kayla was currently struggling financially as a single mother and had no money to invest in her future. She was living off the child support money that her ex-husband was ordered to pay.

When Joyce heard the excitement in her daughter's voice and saw how serious Kayla was to jump start a new journey, she non-hesitatingly volunteered to pay for the course.

Six months later, Kayla completed the course and became a license Real Estate Agent. While attending school she continued to be a faithful member at her church. Reading the word of God was still comforting to her and gave her strength. Her relationship with God was much stronger than ever before. Shortly, after completing the course she built a small home office.

"Kayla! You have a client on the phone, honey." Joyce whispered from the door to her bedroom which also served as a home office. "Can you hold for me, Carrie?" Kayla interrupted the person who she was talking to on her cell phone and put a hand on her speaker. "Mom, ask them to hold for a moment, I'll be right there." "Okay, sweetie." Joyce smiled and left. "Hey, Carrie. So sorry about that." She held her cellphone back to her ear. "And yes, as I said, there are several locations I have in mind for where your salon would be perfect. Let me know when you're free and we can set up a meeting to take a look at them."

After the conversation was over, she took a deep sigh and sat back in her seat before remembering she had another client waiting for her on the landline. Only a few months into her career as a real estate agent, she had been blossoming. Her reviews were impeccable and people trusted her. Her career was thriving more than she ever expected. Had to be the blessings of God. She reflected on the scripture in the bible from {Ephesians 3:20} *"Now unto Him that is able to do exceeding abundantly above all that we ask or think, according to the power that worketh in us."*

After finishing all her phone calls and arranging her appointments, she sat with her mother on the porch to drink coffee. The sun had set and streetlights had begun to illuminate the neighborhood hood. "Mom, I can't believe how God is blessing me. He has definitely turned things around. I think I should get a real office now." Kayla voiced. "And possibly an assistant." "So your old mom isn't good enough for you?" Joyce chuckled, lightly jabbing Kayla with her elbow. "Mom," Kayla whined. "I'm serious. I had no idea it would go this well. I just wanted to do this as something on the side." "Well, I'm glad. Because this is the best thing you could have done. You glow differently now." Joyce commented. "You have become such a strong, independent young woman and you owe it all to yourself."

Kayla's eyes stung as her heart filled with unexplainable emotion. She was proud of herself. In the past years, she had lifted herself and now started seeing her true worth. After feeling like an outcast her whole life, she had polished her strengths and shredded off her insecurities. Now, she spoke with confidence. She stood tall and no longer felt crippling fear before doing something risky. And as her mother said, she owed it all to herself.

"Marcella!" Kayla called out from where she stood in the foyer, a lunchbox in her hand as she tapped her foot waiting for her daughter to come downstairs. "I'm coming, mommy." An annoyed voice replied. "I'm just getting my pink backpack." "Well, hurry up!" She yelled back.

"Why is there so much yelling in the house so early in the morning?" Joyce emerged from the kitchen of their new home. It was two weeks after Marcella's fifth birthday and her first day of kindergarten. Marcella stepped down the stairs one by one in her pigtails and carrying her bright pink backpack, she thought back to her own first day at school and how full of heartbreak it had been. Kayla heard a sniffle from her right and felt tears well in her own eyes. She knew her mother was having the same thoughts as her. Kayla and Joyce dropped Marcella off at her school on her first day together. This first day was different from her own. This one was all smiling and great memories. They both watched Marcella hop off to the front gates to meet her teacher. She turned back once to wave at her mother and grandmother who both sent her prayers in their hearts.

Seven months into Kayla's career, she had definitely turned the corner financially as a real estate agent and was able to purchase her first home and now her mother was residing with her. This house was much bigger and nicer than their old two bedroom shack where she had lived with her mother since she was a child. That house felt like a home, but they could no longer deny that the seepage wasn't bothering them or that the recurring termite issue was something they kept wanting to invest in getting fixed.

So they took the plunge and moved into the better part of the city. They each had their own rooms in this one. There was a beautiful garden in the backyard and the floors were marble. Besides, they would make it feel like home as long as they were all together. Kayla couldn't deny that leaving the old house had helped to shed away the last bits of the bad memories she associated with her childhood.

Kayla lived her life sidelined by society. She was pushed aside by all the men in her life but now she had realized that the only one whose validation she needed in her life was God's. Ever since she had started to rely more on herself and God. Things had started to go well for her, much better than she ever expected. She became more self-confident and blossomed in her personal, professional and spiritual life.

She was no longer alone but had sincere, loving friends and a perfect family in the form of her beautiful mother and loving daughter. That was all she needed. Relying on the love of the men in her life had brought her nothing but despair. But relying on God and God alone made her realize she was fearfully and wonderfully made within herself, who did not need another person to feel worthy.

CHAPTER 8

THE ACT OF FORGIVENESS

Bearing graciously with one another, and willingly forgiving each other if one has a cause of complaint against another; just as the Lord has forgiven you, so should you forgive.

~ Colossians 3:13 | AMP

A knock on her office door snapped Kayla out of her trance. She was engrossed in editing a contract for one of her clients, typing away on her computer in her medium-sized, comfortable office in the city. Her assistant Julia entered the room, file in hand and a small post-it note that she was squinting at. "Kayla, someone named Mr. Scott is on the phone for you. He says it's important." Julia narrated. "What do you want me to tell him?"

Kayla sighed. It had been six years since she last heard from Scott. Surprisingly the mention of him no longer sent her heart into a frenzy anymore. She remembered the time she had spent shrouded in despair where she blamed herself for the longest time, even after she claimed to have recovered. But going through all that she did in the past six years had made her stronger. Stronger than she has ever been. Besides, she had God by her side. She had always had Him by her side. But now, her faith was stronger and it strengthened her from the inside out.

"No, I'll take the call. Thank you, Julia." Kayla said as she picked up the receiver. Julia nodded and left the office. "Hello, Scott," Kayla answered, nonchalantly, flipping through the pages of the contract she was editing while looking at the revisions she made on the screen in front of her. "Kayla! Hey, how are you?" Scott answered. Kayla could hear the smile in his voice. He sounded fresh and light. Good for him, I suppose? Kayla thought. "I'm great. Is there something you need?" Kayla answered, straight forward, and to the point. "I'm busy with work, actually." "Come on, Kayla," Scott whined playfully. It irritated her a little but she brushed it off. "It's been so long. I didn't even know you had an office now. Joyce told me about it."

Upon Kayla's silence, he coughed to clear his throat and began speaking again. This time, she could hear slight nervousness in his voice. "I wanted to ask about Marcella. I called to tell you that," He coughed again. "I'm actually flying over next week so I was thinking I could pick her up–and take her to the amusement park and spend the day with her." "She's never met you before," Kayla replied, politely but a bit confused. "Well, I'm still her dad and I was granted visitation rights." He said, his tone turning defensive. "You shouldn't have a problem with me meeting my own daughter."

"Scott you just can't magically appear after 6 years

My Tears Are in His Hands

and demand to see your daughter. I have to give this some thought." Kayla said with concern. "Come on Kayla! I'm really sorry. I know I acted unseemly but I'm asking for you to forgive me. I realize the mistakes I made by abandoning you and our daughter and I want a chance to make it right. I want to meet her. Please!" Kayla silently shook her head. "Okay, see you next week then."

Next week arrived quickly and Kayla paced the kitchen nervously. Joyce observed her from the side and then glanced at Marcella who was sitting on the living room couch playing a game on her computer. She shook her head and touched Kayla's arm. "You've got nothing to be nervous about dear." She stated. "He's just taking her out for a day. He promised to have her back by sundown." "But-" Kayla attempted to speak. "No buts." Joyce interrupted. "You're nervous because it's their first time meeting. Unless..." Joyce said uncertainly. Kayla looked up questioningly. "Unless?" Joyce looked at her daughter with a sad expression. "Oh. Kayla, I know it must be hard seeing him again for you too." Kayla sighed. "No, mom. I'm fine about that. Honestly. Just worried for Marcella."

The doorbell rang. Kayla and Joyce gave each other a knowing look before smiling. It was going to be okay.

Marcella spent the whole day with her father and Scott returned her to Kayla by sundown as promised. She watched from the window and he opened the door to the car and helped Marcella out of her seat in his rental car. Marcella had a big smile on her face and a bag of candies in her hands. She watched as Marcella hugged her father goodbye and walked back to the house. Scott watched her go inside before getting back into the car and driving away.

Kayla greeted Marcella and asked about her day. Marcella burst into a long rant about how wonderful her day had been. Her eyes were lit up as she spoke about the wonderful time she spent with her father. Kayla's heart was content. She had been skeptical but now that she saw that Marcella was happy, she was less opposed to Scott attempting to build a relationship with her. She had learned a valuable lesson. Kayla had worked very hard to be independent and not to rely on the men in her life. Despite that, she knew what the Holy Bible said about forgiveness – forgiveness is about goodness and extending mercy to those who have harmed us. She also knew that a father's love is essential.

No matter how Scott had wronged her, she was thrilled he was trying to be good to his daughter. But it didn't stop Kayla from pondering why? Afterwards, it was discovered that Scott fell ill after their divorce and his illness made him infertile. He also married again but was unable to have any more children and ultimately his second wife left him. Kayla knew that must have made him realize what a gift from God Marcella was. Scott was alone, infertile and Marcella was all he had now. He had lost everything good in his life and he was the only one to blame.

She recollected about everything she had gone through over the past six years since Scott left them. Kayla realized that after six years he was finally owning up to his mistakes and had made an attempt to rectify the situation. Subsequently, Marcella had gained something her mother Kayla never had, her father. Kayla never wanted her daughter to feel the pain she experienced by not having her father's love and care. She never wanted her daughter to live with the feeling of rejection and harbor the pain as she did. Miraculously, Kayla prayers were answered when Scott reunited with his beloved daughter.

Kayla learned in church that no matter how much pain and suffering she had gone through, that everything was working in her favor. She was grateful that God had mercy on her and healed every part of her brokenness, loneliness and low self-esteem. She knew to remain in a place of peace, restoration and strength she had to do one of the most difficult things – to forgive.

Forgiveness is always hard when we are dealing with deep trauma and pain. However, she knew she had to make a conscious decision to let go negative feelings, anger, resentment that she had for her ex-husband and to forgive him for everything he had done. Her heart was at ease because she was forgiving and had a sincere heart. Her strength had led to her bravery and now she was one of God's strongest soldiers.

APPENDIX A

WHO YOU ARE IN CHRIST

Why is it important to know who you are in Christ?

You need to know who you are in Christ so that you can live a life as God has intended for you in order to fulfill your destiny. Therefore, I encourage you to learn to see yourself as God sees you.

The following Bible verses reveals your identity in Christ:

~ I AM A CHILD OF GOD

The Spirit itself beareth witness with our spirit, that we are the children of God.

{Romans 8:16}

~ I AM LOVED

The Lord hath appeared of old unto me, saying, Yea, I have loved thee with an everlasting love: therefore with loving kindness have I drawn thee.

{Jeremiah 31:3}

~ I AM ACCEPTED

To the praise of the glory of his grace, wherein he hath made us accepted in the beloved.

{Ephesians 1:6}

~ I AM AN OVERCOMER

For whatsoever is born of God overcometh the world: and this is the victory that overcometh the world, even our faith.

{1 John 5:4}

~ I AM CHOSEN

But ye are a chosen generation, a royal priesthood, an holy nation, a peculiar people; that ye should shew forth the praises of him who hath called you out of darkness into his marvellous light.

{1 Peter 2:9}

~ I AM FEARFULLY AND WONDERFULLY MADE

For thou hast possessed my reins: thou hast covered me in my mother's womb. I will praise thee; for I am fearfully and wonderfully made: marvellous are thy works; and that my soul knoweth right well.

{Psalm 139:13-14}

~ I AM MORE THAN A CONQUEROR

Nay, in all these things we are more than conquerors through him that loved us.

{Romans 8:37}

~ I AM JOINT HEIRS WITH JESUS

And if children, then heirs; heirs of God, and joint-heirs with Christ; if so be that we suffer with him, that we may be also glorified together.

{Romans 8:17}

~ I AM UNITED WITH GOD AS ONE SPIRIT

But he that is joined unto the Lord is one spirit.

{1 Corinthians 6:17}

~ I AM A TEMPLE OF GOD

What? know ye not that your body is the temple of the Holy Ghost which is in you, which ye have of God, and ye are not your own?

{1 Corinthians 6:19}

~ I AM A MEMBER OF CHRIST'S BODY

Now ye are the body of Christ, and members in particular.

{1 Corinthians 12:27}

~ I AM REDEEMED AND FORGIVEN

In whom we have redemption through his blood, even the forgiveness of sins.

{Colossians 1:14}

~ I AM COMPLETE IN JESUS CHRIST

And ye are complete in him, which is the head of all principality and power.

{Colossians 2:10}

~ I AM FREE OF CONDEMNATION

There is therefore now no condemnation to them which are in Christ Jesus, who walk not after the flesh, but after the Spirit.

{Romans 8:1}

~ I AM A NEW CREATION

Therefore if any man be in Christ, he is a new creature: old things are passed away; behold, all things are become new.
{2 Corinthians 5:17}

~ I AM ESTABLISHED, ANOINTED, AND SEALED BY GOD

Now he which stablisheth us with you in Christ, and hath anointed us, is God.
{2 Corinthians 1:21}

~ I DO NOT HAVE A SPIRIT OF FEAR

For God hath not given us the spirit of fear; but of power, and of love, and of a sound mind.
{2 Timothy 1:7}

ABOUT THE AUTHOR

My name is Tamika D. Roberson and I was born and raised in St. Petersburg, Florida. I am the only child of a phenomenal woman and the proud mother of one loving son. I grew up fatherless and for years were immersed in pain. Throughout my youthful years I desired my father's love and affection. I felt insecure and shattered at a young age but reclaimed my power as an adult.

As an adult, I had to nurture the wounded girl I once was and embrace my pain and emotions for healing to take place. I have a burning desire to tell women who are hurting that there is a way to heal from their pain. I aim to inspire and encourage young women like myself to be successful women who dream big and achieve their personal, professional and spiritual goals.

I am a graduate of Florida Metropolitan University and has an Associate Degree in Medical Assistant. Shortly after, I enlisted in the United States Air Force and worked as Security Forces, which is the ground combat force and military police for the United States Air Force. I served 4 years active duty and 4 years inactive duty. During my military career I gained my disciplinary and leadership skills. After my military service I worked for the Department of Veterans Affairs for 15 years providing a variety of benefits and services to veterans and their families.

I discovered a passion for event design during my latter years at the Department of Veterans Affairs. After retiring, I pursued my career as an event designer full time. I am a highly motivated, dedicated, and ambitious entrepreneur with an aspiration to plan, organize and design any type of event.

I have faithfully served in ministry for 12 years providing spiritual support to the body of Christ. While seeking the spirit of the Lord I began to unveil the wholeness God has for me, that is when I realized that no one except God has the power to complete me. I count it my greatest privilege to serve and worship the Lord.